# A BRIEF THEORY OF TRAVEL AND THE DESERT

# A BRIEF THEORY OF TRAVEL AND THE DESERT

CRISTIAN CRUSAT

*Translated from the Spanish*
*by Jacqueline Minett*

Hispabooks Publishing, S. L.
Madrid, Spain
www.hispabooks.com




Published by special arrangement with Meucci Agency, Milan
Originally published in Spain as *Breve teoría del viaje y el desierto* by
Editorial Pre-Textos, 2011
First published in English by Hispabooks, 2016


ISBN 978-84-944262-3-0 (trade paperback)
ISBN 978-84-944262-4-7 (ebook)
Legal Deposit: M-23491-2016

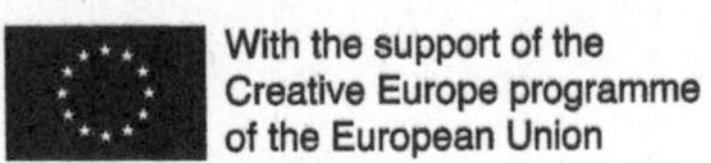


The European Commission support for the production of this publication does not constitute an endorsement of the contents which reflects the views only of the authors, and the Commission cannot be held responsible for any use which may be made of the information contained therein.

*For Rocío*

*Ainsi l'âme va d'un extrême à l'autre,*
*de l'expansion de sa propre vie*
*à l'expansion de la vie de tous*
MARCEL SCHWOB, *Coeur doublé*

*(. . .) como el remolino*
*de dos granos de arena (. . .)*
JOSÉ MORENO VILLA, *Jacinta la Pelirroja*

*Walked hundred miles of desert sun,*
*To grasp the chance that I'll be gone,*
*Be one with you, yeah.*
KYUSS, *Blues for the Red Sun*

# CAMPSITES

I wake up in a daze, drenched in sweat. To my left, Nola and Hazel are still sleeping side by side. Gradually I see them returning from whatever uninhabited zone they've been in, making little moaning noises and getting their revenge by landing me the occasional malicious, resentful kick in the crotch.

"I think I've had that dream again," I say, even though I know nobody gives a damn.

I can't see a thing. As I clamber out of bed, they sprawl and fill the space I leave vacant, like two sisters in their parents' empty bed. I don't know what time it is, but my dulled senses (right now, all my nerve endings lead to an armored bunker lined with thick sheets of cork) tell me that the hands on the clock must form some angle between three and five in the morning. Not bothering to button my shirt, I pat my chest to make sure that the pack of cigarettes is still there.

I grope my way toward the door of the camper. The sheets, unnecessary in this stifling heat, are lying in a heap on the floor. Since we arrived in the desert, my knees make a loud crack whenever I get up. I'm growing old, but I'm not resentful about anything—except for the nuclear accident at Three Mile Island, red mercury and asbestos. My still sleep-drugged sense of touch steers me around a couple of glasses lying on the floor. Using my back and my elbows I feel my way along the linoleum-covered walls, squeezing past the plastic chairs and table. For a moment I think I can see one of the girls sitting on the edge of the bed, her shoulders rigid as if she were sitting at a misty piano. But she isn't. She never is.

I don't know how many days it's been since I saw the sun, holed up in the RV every day until the early hours of the morning. It must be at least four days since Nola did her dance in front of the pyre of toothless animals.

Outside, the peace and quiet of the place is a stark contrast to my fitful dreams, with their sudden free falls into the void, grim cattle markets, and members of my family in humiliating situations. I go out into the suffocating night air and walk around our site in the deserted campground; it's about the size of a small barn. The night opens up before me like the rusty zipper on a pair of old 501 jeans. There's nothing but scorched earth. And mosquitoes with their promise of impending doom in the hostile shadows. Getting my bearings, I stretch my legs and head toward the front of our camper. Before mulling over the night's events, I decide to light up a cigarette. Leaning against the still hot vent, my eyes begin to make out the garbage that has been thrown at our vehicle. There are condoms strewn among the hanging laundry, others dangling from the rearview mirror, and even some on the side window, sticking to the screen. "They've been used," I say to myself, blowing out the match. On the matchbox, I read the words ARMANDO'S FISH & CHIPS. Quickly glancing around me, by the meager light from the match as its glow fades in the darkness, I see that the lights in the other vehicles and campers are all turned off. A phosphorescent glow hugs the horizon of ridges, ravines, and hills. The counties to the east of our campground have vanished from view. Only the outline of the water tank stands out in the distance against the uniform blackness of the night, with its intolerable stench of gasoline and semen. It is so hot that I imagine campfires burning in this dark old southern sky.

I sit down on the bottom step of the trailer. Inevitably, I think about the quarrel we had this evening, and about the way I behaved. I can't say I'm proud of it. And I'd rather not remember the things I said: *I don't need any other women. I have enough with two of you. I'm no hero! When will you get that into your heads?* By the time I got back, they were sprawled out fast asleep on the bed, leaving no room for me. And then there were those nightmares.

I run the burning end of my cigarette around the latex rim of a condom that is clinging to a scorpion-shaped rock still hot from the afternoon sun.

"It makes great glue," I think to myself.

Suppressing the urge to throw up, I focus on my feelings of guilt about everything that happened tonight: fire rips through an undergrowth of vigorous, lush vegetation inside me, like a landscape in an old black-and-white photograph burning on contact with the invisible bonfires that fill the air.

I hate these feelings and the way they transform into absurd nightmares.

"Don't worry, Olivieri," says a voice to my right. It is a sexless voice, thin as a red-hot silver thread. Unable to see a thing, I'm startled and brace myself for some hideous object to be thrown at me. "It was one of those gangs of Cajun boys that did it—four or five little hoodlums with shaved heads."

After trying for a few seconds to adapt to night vision, I make out the figure of our neighbor sitting beside the trailer to the right of ours. It's as if she has sprung from some dark recess of the nightmare that kept me awake tonight. She reminds me of those nocturnal beings who lie in wait at crossroads and borders, on wasteland and in dense forests, and are especially dangerous if they see you before you see them. She has been here ever since we arrived at the campground. She is always the first one here. Nobody—but nobody—talks to her. I stand and start to button up my shirt, still not seeing her clearly. My left sleeve hangs like an empty drainpipe.

"Oh, yes . . . Good evening, ma'am."

Nola is a little frightened of her because she reminds her of her aunt in Denver, the one who is sick with pellagra. And Hazel thinks she is "as creepy as a jar of jam on a sports wheelchair."

She is sitting in a rocking chair, between a stinking diesel oil drum and that rickshaw contraption where animals go to hide away, languish and die. She doesn't answer, so I say, "Is the heat keeping you awake, too?"

A small flash of light darts across my campsite and touches base between my neighbor's legs. I can just make out its tail. It's her disgusting, fat, crippled cat, heading home through the garbage piled up in front of our trailer. Carrying a banana peel in its mouth, it scuttles away to hide behind one of the four blocks of concrete supporting my neighbor's camper: a tuna boat stranded in the middle of this stretch of the Arizona desert that has no zip code.

"Fine night, ain't it?" she asks in a distinctive southern accent, drawling her words the way I've heard some sheepshearers talk. "A welcome change after such a hot day."

I nod without knowing what to say. I'm used to not arguing with women. Everything is so dark . . . I recall that someone, somewhere, paid seven dollars for two pounds of wool . . . Every now and then, due to an optical illusion brought on by fatigue, I see sudden flashes on the horizon, like the faint glimmering of myriad knives and hatchets in the sky over this desert, as empty as an abandoned rooftop. I can only see a couple of yards beyond my neighbor, and then nothing.

For no particular reason, I randomly think of a country—Tunisia. It has a desert, too.

"At least people have stopped throwing trash at our trailer," I say and immediately regret it before finishing the sentence. Except for those condoms, of course . . . all that withered, rancid life enveloped in darkness. "What I mean is . . ."

"Yeah, I know. All those . . . *things*. I sure am sorry about that."

"It's okay. We're leaving tomorrow," I say, clumsily trying to change the subject.

"Will you be staying long?" I ask, sounding inquisitive without intending to be. So then I try to play it down (sometimes I forget my Jewish roots) by saying "Not in that rocking chair, of course, I meant the campground."

There's nothing to suggest it. Or, then again, maybe there is . . . Those concrete blocks are like an accent or an asterisk earmarking her life, singling her out as a "permanent resident." She must be about ten or fifteen years older than me. She might already be seventy, although she doesn't look it. I couldn't say for sure how old she is. She's always sitting there in her rocking chair, as if she were convalescing, like everyone else here. And yet, I can see she has a good, firm bone structure, which tends to betoken at least a gradual, dignified decline.

"Quite a while, I reckon. Quite a while."

I don't pursue the matter. I think I can hear one of the girls calling me. Perhaps it's Nola who can't find the pee bucket. Or Hazel, who is feeling hungry or sick. *I don't need any other women. I have enough with two of you.* I take a look inside the camper and light another of those matches from ARMANDO'S, fish and pancakes in the foothills of the Rincon Mountains. Fortunately, everything is quiet. Otherwise, the situation would get worse. Very gently, I close the door with its aluminum rivets running down each side. This silence (an empty, hollowed-out silence that contains neither echoes nor omens) emphasizes the lateness of the hour.

"I was wondering if we disturbed you," I begin to apologize quietly, too quietly, fearing the mere sound of my voice might push up the temperature. "If we did, I'm sorry . . . That is, all three of us are sorry. We've had a few disagreements."

"You're pouring water into a bottomless pitcher," comes her voice, out of the darkness.

It goes without saying that I have no idea what she's talking about.

So I decide not to answer that.

"I guess our walls are not very thick."

*A bottomless pitcher?*

"No, they're not," she replies. Neither of us says anything for a moment.

"Why don't you move a bit closer?" she says, just before I start to feel really uncomfortable, which is when she says, "We'll wake them up if we keep talking at this distance."

Nevertheless, I have to admit she's right. In any case, I think to myself, I'm past feeling tired. It's going to be another sleepless night. I figure I've gotten used to our nocturnal conversations—impersonal, anonymous, superfluous . . . puzzling. I remember living for a time with a woman called Serena who could talk until dawn. It was in Oakland, right above a car dealership. All the stories she told were about Irish bars and the evenings in those Irish bars. She used to chat away, and I would nod and look out the window at the hoods of the cars, while down below some prospective buyer pushed back the seat of a Mazda coupé or measured the trunk with a pink tape measure. Underlying all that was what we usually call *time*.

I do as she suggests, true to the ritual of the last few days, like an unexceptional chess player sitting down opposite a stranger—a friendly, worldly-looking rabbi—and starting to play in some park or other, surrounded by yellowish ash trees and lesbian skaters jabbering in Russian. Stubbing out my cigarette against the scorpion-shaped rock, I stand up, trying to work out where I'm going to sit. Once I'm on my feet, I can't decide between one of the concrete blocks, one of my folding chairs, or the hard ground. Through the beads of sweat on my eyelashes, I see the landscape not as it is, but as an enlarged, distorted reflection of the landscape, like the image you see on the silvery surface of a bauble hanging from a Christmas tree. At last, I start to walk toward her, stupidly trying to delay making the decision. It's a dumb move, I know, but it helps me as I work my way through these feelings that border on guilt. I stumble several times over two soda cans that I didn't see. I lose my balance and lean my shoulders against something, I don't know what. I think she is looking the other way so as not to embarrass me. Deducing that I pose a threat, the cat squeals, sounding more like a rat. I end up sitting, as I always knew I would, on one of the concrete blocks, the one nearest our RV, even though from here I can smell the stench of warmed-up spunk surrounded by a swarm of insects. I have rather long legs, and the position I'm sitting in is not very natural, to put it mildly. From our row of trailers on one of the highest points in the campground, I can make out the canopy of skylights, solar panels, and metal rivets that slope down to the neon arch in the shape of bull's horns, its glow lighting up a small cloud of dust about three hundred yards away. The campground is surrounded by wire fencing. Beyond that (again, I note, without the slightest interest or concern), there is nothing. To tell the truth, I can't imagine what nothing is.

"They sounded very upset," she says.

Before answering, I resign myself to the fact that this is what fate has in store for me, at least tonight. Here I am again, talking to her in the dark, with the condoms, the heat, the bottomless pitcher . . . For a moment I forget the nightmare in which I see my father, clutching his oxygen tank and riding a pony on an old fairground carousel; then, hanging onto the animal's amorphous dick—now it's a real live pony, not a papier-mâché one—he spirals into the void. Considering my origins, these dreams are obviously my own small contribution to the Jewish guilt trip. I spit out the persistent, lip-cracking dust, parting my knees so that the gobbet of spit can pass between my legs. From the concrete block opposite, the cat has started to make low threatening noises. It's staring at my left sleeve that flaps about as I move. So I strike a match to see where the animal is and ward off its evil designs on my person, but I end up lighting another cigarette.

"It's Hazel. She's indignant about the way folks treat us on this campground," I say.

"I heard everything, Olivieri. There's no need to explain."

"But that's what it was all about," I protest in an offended voice. "You just have to look at our site . . . Nola . . . she doesn't even . . ."

"Nola?"

"The tall, blond one with the beekeeper's mask. She's just a girl . . ."

"I'm not one to poke my nose in other folks' business, but your caterwauling could be heard as far away as West Tucson. I reckon everybody between here and there must know about your doings. And anyway, you only have to look at the state of your campsite . . . It's filthy . . ."

I've got my eye on the cat. It's as if it were the cat talking to me through its whiskers. "The filth just keeps mounting up, like what you said about Rachel's indignation . . ."

"*HAZEL!*" I shout, wondering what the hell she's talking about. If that cat comes any closer, I'll kick it or stub my cigarette out on its slanting eyes. "Is it sick? Is there something wrong with it?"

"I gotta hand it to you."

"Huh?"

"I said, I gotta hand it to you. They're real pretty. I know, because they always walk around naked."

"Oh yeah, thanks," I concur.

"As for you, you're not getting any younger, and you only have one arm . . ."

"Uh, yeah, well . . ."

"Next time, I'd close your door, if I were you."

I say nothing.

"What's that thing for, that Nola wears on her head?" she pipes up again, not surprising me in the least.

If we weren't in the dark, I think I'd be offended. But it's like I'm talking to the desert itself, I'm actually managing to put my feelings into words, and that makes me feel better.

"It's to protect her against radiation. Electricity, power lines, transmission towers, hidden radio waves . . . It saps her energy." Fortunately, the cat has decided to call a truce—strange for a cat that literally thrives on our insults. "Cell phones are the worst of all."

Feeling calmer now that the animal is no longer a threat, I explain to her again that we have come here, among other reasons, because this square mile southwest of nowhere is one of the rare places where there is still no wireless phone service —a dead zone. Just one of the strange places we live in for a time. *I'm no hero.* I can't even pinpoint the origin of all this, or put my finger on where it began. I also tell her that we don't have a television, a radio, a telephone, or a computer . . . or any of the things that send Nola's nervous system—and, by extension, Hazel's and my own—into meltdown. Evidently, she and all the other inhabitants of the campground—most of them eaten up with greed, poverty, and AIDS (which makes their prophylactic ballistics even more sinister) are also cut off from the world, although in her case it seems to be because she likes it that way. All we wanted was gasoline and a place with no telephone signal before we continued our journey.

When I have finished explaining all this, she politely excuses herself as she slowly and painfully gets up from her rocking chair. Now, for the first time, I can see her entire body from close up. I am usually the one to end our conversations, which are identical night after night: the filthy state of our campsite, how pretty Hazel and Nola are, their boundless, misplaced love for me, the reasons for our peregrinations to get away from any electric currents . . . Perhaps that is why she says nothing about herself. Then she's gone, and with her, once more, her crystal-clear memory. Is it possible that I am the first person on this campground to see her like this? She is average height and, as I guessed, her frame is pretty sturdy. So, her fragility must stem from some other part of her being, from some hidden recess of her inner self . . . from her proximity to death, perhaps, I wonder for no particular reason. I don't know the cause of her apparent thinness. She is temperamental, and she has a magnetic personality, I can feel it, and (despite the overbearing heat and my fatigue) I can't get away from her or her compelling force of will. Day after day, the same gestures and conversations are repeated. What is it about her that is so mesmerizing? And why is she here, among all these wretched souls in the middle of the desert? (Where the smell is foul and hope has run out.) Without fear of being mistaken, I say to myself that at least she is not sick—unlike the rest of this community. How do I know? It's obvious from her wrists. The first symptom of illness always shows in the wrists: fragile, brittle, an unhealthy whitish color . . . Like fish caught in a net, twitching and exhausted. But she is not like that. In fact, the more I think about it, the younger she seems to get. Living purely in the present. A woman who is in control of her place in the world, unbent by fate in so many ways. Unlike myself, who is doomed to pour water into a bottomless pitcher. As she climbs the steps to her camper, I study her feet, her hips, her long graying hair that tumbles rebelliously to her waist, like an old girlfriend with whom you are reunited after a long separation (as you clutch a carton of spoiled milk with an unrecognizable photo of her printed on it). She hasn't turned on the light, so I can't see what she does once she is inside.

Around the campground you can still see the entrances to the old nuclear bomb shelters. As we had some time to kill over the past few days, I visited them with the same solemn interest normally reserved for the ancient sites of Mesopotamia or Cyprus. I'm told they were converted into underground studios by artists—constructivist sculptors whose parents cashed in on their real estate to swap New York for some place in the Mid-West. That's the way it is round here. And she's the only one who calls me Olivieri.

I make the most of her brief absence to think about what she said and stretch my legs. They are stiff from sitting in that uncomfortable position. I move toward the trailer, picking my way between the peels, the condoms, and the occasional sanitary pad. I can't hear anything. I kick the trailer tires with my leather boots, raising a miniature dust devil that swirls around my ankles. *She* doesn't pour water into a bottomless pitcher. She thinks she *is* the water. *Will you ever understand?* For a moment, I'm tempted to turn on the ignition and get out of here right now in the middle of the night, while the girls and my neighbor are fast asleep. That would be truly heroic, but only superficially. While I am considering this possibility, the lights suddenly go up on the carousel that I have seen my father riding every night since we arrived here. The light bulbs decorating the revolving platform of the carousel come on one by one, projecting at the base of each animal a grid of uniform shadows over which the image of my father and his damn oxygen tank constantly flicker. His pony, the only one that isn't made of papier-mâché, is hanging by its neck from a *pink* synthetic rope, and it is urinating its pain. The puddle from the stream is about to overflow and fuse one of the tungsten light filaments. Then everything blacks out again. This time, my father has been saved from the void. (I am profoundly relieved: given my present age, I am actually *older* than he is so it is my duty to protect him.) I smile to myself. As I head back toward my neighbor's trailer, feeling much better for having kept my father from danger, I mutter something to get the cat's attention. It approaches me from its hiding place behind the rickshaw and rubs its frail spine against my ankle.

"Are we friends now?" I whisper.

I'd have no qualms about filling its balls with buckshot . . . Meanwhile, my neighbor has come back and sat down in the rocking chair. I walk over to her and sit down on the same concrete block as before. Another phosphorescent light streaks across the sky, and for one long moment the horizon fleetingly resembles a photographer's darkroom.

"I think I know what you meant when you said I was *pouring water into a bottomless pitcher.*"

Something stirs beneath her feet.

"Is that so? I'm glad, very glad," she replies animatedly.

"Yes, yes, I really do," I say. And I launch a discreet attack, an innocent little ambush. I can't repress a burning wave of latent euphoria rising in me because of the discovery I have just made.

"Pouring water into a bottomless pitcher." It's all to do with the *time* we live in. It's plain to see that in her case time doesn't fly. It just repeats itself over and over again.

"Do you always spend all night in your rocking chair?" I ask. "Don't you ever sleep, for Pete's sake?"

This is our last night here, after all, and here I am pouring that water . . . Endlessly pouring water . . . Day and night. Just like she said. Every night, in the small hours of the morning, my father rides my nightmare carousel and hovers on the edge of the void, but tonight I have kept him safe.

She doesn't answer. But I don't think I've offended her. A few seconds pass before either of us speaks. It is not an awkward silence, and I wonder, who is she, who is this woman who knows me so well, and how can she possibly know me? It is only the *bottomless* silence of the desert. Everybody should experience it.

Until now I have never attributed my neighbor's absences to any external cause. Perhaps she has gone in to unscrew an orthopedic leg or cough up a blob of blood as big as a calf's heart, big enough to choke her if she doesn't spit it out. Or perhaps she has a gun hidden away in a drawer and, finally, this is the day she is going to kill me. God only knows why I am obsessed with her enigmatic state of health. I think I see a shadow moving inside her camper. The shady figure of a hunched-up man with a shriveled face, like the overcooked white of a fried egg. "How about that!" I think to myself. "Now that's a surprise." But it doesn't matter anymore. Suddenly I realize what she has gone inside to do. The reason lies in the dark interior of her trailer. It is so long since I heard music, isolated as we are from any electrical appliances or aerials, that it takes me a moment to identify the sound that startled me. It has been playing softly for several minutes, a lulling sound in the half-light that shrouds the silhouettes on the horizon. My neighbor is stroking her fat, crippled cat in time to the music, listening to the melody with such careful concentration that she seems to sense the ineffable moment when the music settles on each grain of sand, each mesquite bush, like a single bee pollinating a vast fragrant field of violets. The music is like a fine, fertilizing rain under whose touch this tough, dry campground full of electronic outcasts shimmies and trembles. I sense the presence of the male figure; he looks at me and scurries out of sight. I don't know who he is, but the smell of shit starts to drift toward me. I can't remember the last audio system I had or what make it was, whether it was a CD or a cassette player . . . Whether I bought it in Singapore or Pennsylvania, whether I was with Serena, Sherry, or Svetlana or some other girl at the time, before my life with Hazel and Nola, far from all sources of radiation . . . I don't even know what type of music it is. What I mean is that I can't identify it, but it makes everything seem very real. It is sad and happy at the same time, both consoling and unfathomable. A few scorpions approach us, forming a strange and dangerous audience. Their shadows etch an indecipherable code in the sand, a mosaic of menace.

I have to get back. I can't stay any longer. My neighbor has obviously forgotten that I am here. In a gesture intended to mark a break with my surroundings, I light another cigarette as I watch the dawn warming the horizon again.

"Have a good day," I murmur in farewell, and then I stand up and go back to my own campsite.

Don't ask me why, but as I make my way back to our camper, the music—with a melody that reminds me of the "methamphetamine blues"—makes me think it's the song of the last human left on Earth: taking stock of his extraordinary circumstances, he walks a few yards, pauses to look at the soles of his shoes, and then maybe swats away some sort of fly or plucks a hair from the mole next to his right nipple. That is the extent of the surviving technology. After a long while, he looks at his body. Then he continues to walk, and all around him there are bright flashes, fragments of broken mirrors and tiny particles of sand and ash. He knows that, minute by minute, he is crumbling into dust, and he knows that it is magnificent. Later, he sits down. The last man on Earth, and he's sitting down. The heat has vanished from the surface of the Earth. There is no echo, or perhaps that is all there is. Before singing for the last time, he thinks of his father on that winter afternoon; he thinks of his father's powerful wrists, raising him high toward the warm afternoon sunlight, and much higher still: toward that guilty, unmistakable, urine-colored light.

# FROM LENA TO THE READER OF HER STORY

## (The room of lost footsteps)

Because God appears to us not in our thoughts,
but in our dreams.
There he sits,
waiting to make love with us.
MILORAD PAVIC

I, who in dreams cast no shadow and know no fear; I, who as I walk along an endless tree-lined avenue am a vanishing point destined to disappear in the distance (all the while, dry autumn leaves slowly tumble to the ground); and you: a figure standing by the side of that avenue, leaning against an old wagon under a gray sky, gray as the sky over Paris or Vienna in an old movie; you light a cigarette and then petulantly toss the spent match to the ground.

Cut? Fade to black? And I ask myself, "Do dreams come to an end when somebody decides that they will, right there and then, at their whim?"

That's how it has happened in our case, at least, in this idealized love affair between fiction and reality. And so I imagine that you are dreaming what I have already seen in my solitary nights, that we are fantastically united as if we were falling asleep together between the roots of an old almond tree. It goes without saying that you also would cast no shadow—either in my dreams or, of course, the stories that you gate-crash. But we know that you are a reader of stories and that you readers will never be able to conceal the fact that you are crazy.

Since you vanished from this story that I have always inhabited, my nights have been filled with dreams that not even Inguerina could decipher, no matter how hard she tried; visions through which I walk barefoot, carefully extinguishing all the lights, one by one. Incidentally, in the dream about the avenue at the cemetery that I just mentioned (does it remind you of anyone or anything? Orson Welles, say?) our hats fall to the ground—no, that's a lie: like seed fluff they nonchalantly float on and on, *ad infinitum*, without ever touching the ground—as our mouths press together. Now that I *can* dream (and that is all thanks to you), each night I dream of a succession of rural landscapes with cemeteries overgrown with wild flowers and rampant under-growth, places where amazing fantasies always play out happily for me, a far cry from the depressing cemeteries that readers know out there in the real world, where death may be lurking beneath the touch of every pair of lips.

The meetings every Thursday on the first floor of number 9, Svetozara Radica still take place as usual. They begin a little later now, though, because we all cherish the hope that you will come back one day (all of us, that is, except for that die-hard skeptic Pavle Bornemisza, who has finally given you up for dead or *dissolved*). He is as obsessed as ever with his romantic conquests: last month he started courting a friend of Yautsin's, but only *until* the girl turned into a mermaid after failing to go into mourning for the death of her father. His account of the metamorphosis was heartrending. Nothing of the sort happened, of course, but I caught a distinct whiff of the brine from her fins when we invited him round last week and he told us the story while we were waiting for you, with that powerful gift for storytelling of his that is only comparable to your own (although in your case, it is more a need to lose yourself in the story, a kind of ancestral trancelike state to combat time). The days grow longer and longer now, in contrast to my happiness; sometimes it is still light when we sit down to dinner. Which gives that lying Inguerina an even better chance of a writer one day deciding to tell her story, if that's really what is destined to happen. Whoever would be foolhardy enough to make Inguerina the main character in a story! If you should happen to see my writer again, tell him to hurry up and invent a house for my friend. In the meantime, I suppose I could become a writer and give Inguerina her very own story in which to shelter from life and the fierce wind that blows off the Sava River. After all, we all deserve to have a story because we are all crazy and deserve to die plastered out of our minds.

It must have been last Thursday evening when Inguerina brought along to our gathering two brothers whose story is bound to interest you. Once you've read my letter, you can pass it on to anybody you choose, and feel free to add or omit whatever you like. You see, life is as skittish and playful as a puppy that has fallen into a tub. These two brothers are equal protagonists in the story of the brothers in love, which begins one fleeting spring morning. I'll spare you the full stop, new paragraph. The wind had died down, giving way to a soft breeze, the protean clouds bore witness to the imperfect order of the universe, and the spokes on Inguerina's bicycle glinted in the sunlight as she went on her morning ride. It was then that she saw them: they were crying on each other's shoulders, facing each other on the terrace of one of the cafés next to the National Theater. It must have been a sad sight indeed that met Inguerina's eyes that morning, because she burst into tears, put on her brakes and immediately cut short her bicycle ride. The sky clouded over and her bicycle wheels, suddenly bereft of sunshine and joy, stood motionless. The waiter wept, and a Persian cat mewed at the feet of a drowsy customer, while the parakeet locked in a cage at the entrance of the café flew round and round, constantly crashing against its bars. As if that weren't bad enough, beside the door of the Turkish café there was a huge sack of pepper, from which a detestable smell wafted all over the neighborhood. The waiter, an old man known to everybody, asked Inguerina if she would be kind enough to escort the brothers off the premises, because otherwise their sadness would overwhelm the sun and it would never shine again in Belgrade and all the terrace cafés would have to shut down. So Inguerina turned round and perched on the handlebars, and the two brothers started to pedal in time to their sobs and set off in the direction of my house under a glowering gray sky. One of the brothers was tall with strong arms, thinning blond hair; and his pants couldn't conceal that he was very well endowed, although his voice was too high-pitched for my liking. The other one was much shorter, with a face like a hearty sailor's and, in contrast to his bald brother, he had hair that smelled like honey at breakfast time.

Naturally, they were the first to arrive at the meeting that Thursday, and it is only now that I remember how long ago it was: Ovidian wheels within wheels.

It occurred shortly after you appeared at my house that blessed night that begot two creations (the one of my blood and the other of my dreams). I recall that I was still in the shower, my eyes closed and listening through the steam to the wonderful music of *Jurassic Park* (a strange choice as my signature tune in the world, everybody thinks, and they're right). That very afternoon I had come to the conclusion that there was no bird more literary, no bird more worthy of the storyteller's art (remember that famous poem by Apollinaire?) than the legendary Roc that lays giant eggs in the middle of the desert. Worthier by far than the turtledove, of which Mistress Page in *The Merry Wives of Windsor* said (if my memory serves me correctly) that it would take less time to find twenty lascivious turtledoves than one chaste man. I can't agree with that. Today I saw two men kissing in broad daylight and I was struck by the perfection of the scene: the beginning and end of an ideal world. (Or, perhaps, the opposite: a clever and menacing pre-arranged signal of destruction.)

Reluctantly, the brothers sat down in my living room as far from each other as possible. Was there tension? You can't begin to imagine how much! Inguerina and I went into the kitchen to fix something to eat and my regular guests gradually began to arrive: incredulous Pavle, Yautsin the future publisher, a stuck-up girl without much imagination from the School of Fine Arts and that nymph with an incredible gift for fantasy, although I can't recall if they arrived in that order. They asked after you again and my spirits sank; we waited for you for quite some time until I finally said what I always say: when I woke up, you were no longer there and I had grown very small.

The damp air coming off the Sava that night, together with the hostile presence of the two brothers, had combined to create for the first time at my Thursday gathering a gloomy, ominous atmosphere, a kind of mourning for your diluted reader's soul. We were looking at each other in silence and nibbling unenthusiastically on our food when Inguerina came right out and asked the brothers her stock-in-trade question:

"Tell me, which of you two is the best kisser?"

They stared at each other and started to sob faster than night falls in winter. Until that point they had managed to go for almost an hour without crying.

"The woman I love reigns supreme when it comes to kisses, and each one is unlike all those that went before," said the short, plucky one, looking at his brother with renewed contempt. The latter jumped up and tried to throw him a punch, but he was thwarted in the attempt by a bold move on Pavle's part, which resulted in a bloody nose for the taller of the two. At that point, the stuck-up girl from the School of Fine Arts fainted on my carpet (as if instead of a drop of blood she had seen the image of her own death, now that she had fallen in love).

The short, plucky brother, looking for all the world like a royal equerry, added after a studied dramatic pause (the stuck-up girl blinked again, fluttering her eyelashes with the nonchalant flapping of a butterfly's wings) that the woman he loved above all others had Genoa green eyes (although somewhat envious, I was not familiar with the shade) and a crown of dark hair braided into a wreath. During the above-mentioned pause, we all sketched in our imagination the nude figure of the woman, fleshing out her exquisite attributes as his description progressed. Her long hair reached to her hips, which were firm and supple like those of a Classical Greek female figure. It was a promising start, and I was eager to hear more and forget about you for a while (naturally!). And yet, his story had the saddest of endings. It was an unhappy love story with the unhappiest of partings; the shabby, rustically painted building of a train station: a post-war Yugoslavian train station. That says it all . . . Imagine a waiting room with a checkered tile floor and worm-eaten wooden window frames beside the only door, which rattled in the icy March wind. And a sky which sometimes, and only after the war, turned a shocking pink, like the color of strawberry-flavored chewing gum. The wind whistled and a beggar caught forty winks on one of the benches. The air was thick with the smell of cheap wine on his breath. I shan't go on, because otherwise I'll wax rhetorical—much to my professors' delight. The switchman's signal sounded and everyone got up to leave the waiting room. She said nothing as she walked toward the cramped railroad car. It was only when he looked at her through the window that the brother understood: not only did the woman not love him but she was already madly in love with another man. Made even more beautiful by her treachery and the announcement that the train was about to depart, she waved the silk handkerchief that she always had with her. She was traveling with three suitcases, each one heavier than the last, with the lightest of the three reserved exclusively for hats, gloves, and scarves. The train pulled out of the station, although where it was going the brother did not know. Incredible though it may seem, he didn't know her destination. Like the song says, "*And she's always gone too long, / any time she goes away.*" In a fit of impotence, he tore off his shirtsleeves, exactly as he later did in my living room in front of everybody assembled there. Pretending that the gap between my living room and the kitchen were the misty glass in the railcar window, he took five calculated steps back, thus revealing to all those present what his beloved, and even the stationmaster, had witnessed on the day of the farewell (the whole scene enveloped in the thick mist rising off the Sava!): a magnificent tattoo on his right bicep:

I WILL LOVE YOU ETERNALLY, GISELLE

This is as true as the fact that in his last will and testament Shakespeare bequeathed his second-best bed to his wife, plus—I hasten to add—the corresponding "furniture" or bedding. Now that I mention it, I remember the letters tattooed in mock oblivion green (Genoa green?), faded to the point of almost being erased from his arm as well as my imagination. Looking out the window as I write this, they (the letters and Giselle herself) vanish in the wake of an ambulance that at this very moment crosses my mind as it passes along my street. I also notice that the sorrel in the garden seems to have grown to fill the empty spaces of the night. The ambulance is not coming for me, the blood that pulses in me and beats against my belly is not yet ready to see the light of day. The sound of ambulances is strange, I remember you saying that night of love (you had come into my story and my home for the second and last time). They wail mournfully through the streets of the city that we inhabit, but sound strangely familiar in foreign cities, telling of human tragedies, our own tragedies, with their metallic echo of other people's misfortunes.

Do you want to know how the story of the two brothers ends?

Take from the story whatever moral you please. Add it to my days without you, read it metaphorically and sum up my life. After all, life is the product of other people's dreams, and all we can do is make the best of it in the benevolent darkness.

The love story of the tall, strong, blond brother was just beginning (not without a certain relish for paradox and far-fetched symmetry) in another, faraway Central European train station.

The second brother proved to be a person with next to no imagination, who had absolutely nothing in common with the melancholy equerry, and it takes a greater effort of the imagination on my part to conjure him up. Moreover, he seemed to be ruled by his unattractive baldness, for baldness—like the color of a person's eyes—defines character. His story was different from his brother's. He wasn't there to meet or say goodbye to a girlfriend. He was in low spirits, far from his native Novi Beograd, and hijacked by the asphyxiating machinery of time. He couldn't bear any story—starting with that of his own life—that didn't have a beginning or an end, although we would all be better off if we realized that we are always somewhere in the middle (of time, the hurricane, a story, or the queue at the grocery store). It was not only sadness, but also nostalgia that gripped him and led him to the station that day. Nostalgia for his twenty-two-year-old self, the age of absolute plenitude, when one's hair grows more vigorously and love is resistant to the corrosion of boredom and habit. He was enjoying a day off work from the German ship that had signed him on as a stoker, so he headed for the station in the city where the ship had docked, searching for others as melancholy as himself. He was looking for someone who perhaps had just said farewell to a beloved wife, a deaf-mute orphan looking for a better life, or a newcomer to those parts who might be feeling overwhelmed by the gloomy, inhospitable atmosphere of that place of transit. Above all, he was looking for tears held back but about to break over the floodgates of eyelids reddened by memories. In the midst of all that sad weariness of life, the lips of a woman flooded the station platforms with light as she stepped off the train, illuminating the face of each and every passenger and disoriented passer-by, including that of the brother. And so, on that godforsaken railroad platform, began the love story between the saddest of stokers and that lady with an indefatigable capacity for love, but whose image eludes my exhausted memory tonight like fine sand slipping through one's fingers. It is Wednesday, and for the first time I find myself dislocated from my story, but only for as long as it will take me to finish this letter; and then I shall never leave it again. The story of the two brothers will finish onboard a small dinghy (back home in their native Belgrade, on a once-more navigable Danube), sailing up the river with a woman who says she is leaving for somewhere in Germany, while promising to return. On this occasion it was the tall, strong brother whose brown eyes filled with tears, but he never saw her again.

I felt sorry for the bald, deserted brother, as he stood there on the lonely loading dock; motionless beneath a *chiaroscuro* sky as he despairingly looked on at the ill-defined traces left by love in its permanent flight. It wasn't a feeling of sadness that he harbored in his embittered heart. Imitating the mysterious behavior of the brave little equerry, he got up from his chair, spat out a grape pip he had been chewing, and angrily pulled his left sleeve up as far as his shoulder. The other brother was even more surprised than we were. I was sitting with my back to him, so I tried to look at his arm in the reflection of the mirror in my living room, but that part of his body coincided with the hole in one of the corners of that magic looking glass. As there was no reflection, I thought for a few seconds that he must be another reader who had slipped into the story to visit us.

Then I remembered that you hadn't come that Thursday. The illusion—like the mystery—lasted just a few seconds. Then the spell was broken and I read the second prosaic tattoo of the evening:

YOU'LL PAY FOR THIS, GISELLE

Several minutes passed between the revelation of the vengeful inscription and the tall brother returning to his seat, rolling down his shirtsleeve as he did so. The two brothers stared at one another, recognizing their single, shared misfortune (which was possibly that of having stumbled into this story). Inguerina changed the subject. Improbable though it might seem, at the end of the evening the two brothers joined in a resigned embrace, the most conventional ending you could imagine for a truly crazy story. Oddly enough, stories don't always have surprises in store for us. Sometimes they are as dull as life outside fiction, although, generally speaking, everything is worse out there in your world. But, my dear reader, just tell me one thing. Are the concerts at that new club on Kralja Aleksandra Boulevard, the one next to the Technical College, as good out there as they are in my story? Poor Yautsin is dying to know the answer.

I don't know what else to say . . . Everybody knows I'm useless at goodbyes. Since that night, the meetings in this story of ours have continued to take place every week without anything eventful or worthy of comment taking place. Although we amuse ourselves, routine leads us—Thursday in, Thursday out—to some vague and imprecise full stop, like stories that end in an anticlimax (as a matter of fact, I prefer them to stories with an unexpected twist at the end). Hope also continues to fade, although not my infinite love for you, dear reader. I have given up hope that I'll ever see you again . . . I can only hope that I continue to be visited at night by dreams like those I described at the beginning of this letter, here in this room of forgotten steps with its smell of old pipe tobacco. Your soul got locked away somewhere inside me, circulating in my blood, never sleeping, never still. I could cut out my own tongue to stop telling myself stories, but that would solve nothing. So now you have your letter, and the two brothers have their not very edifying story. I'm afraid poor Inguerina will have to go on waiting. Letters finish when they finish.

# ALIEN

I had suggested several places where we might go for our first vacation as a married couple. I considered the possibility of spending a week on the island of Ischia, of which my only memory was the bitter taste of a fish soup I had eaten there. I also thought about a camping holiday in the Algarve, where I had spent one summer holiday with my aunt and uncle. I even called to inquire about the price of a double room in a B&B on the Frisian Islands, where a colleague in my department had stayed a few months earlier. On his return, he told me about the disquieting experience of seeing the immense curve of the Earth from a beach that stretched miles and miles when the tide was out. He described an eerie *sfumato* of the blue atmosphere fading into the austere darkness of outer space—a rather improbable image, but one which has stayed with me ever since. However, three months before the summer (around the time I was checking the rates of a Dutch B&B), Alien's father moved to the island of I., where the hotel chain he worked for had transferred him after thirty years at the same hotel in Lloret de Mar. So we put our plans on hold for a year and Alien decided we should pay her father a visit, especially as our work at the university had prevented us from giving him a hand with the move. In any case, neither of us had ever been there. She took her holidays early and promised to be back in the office at the end of August, before the rest of her colleagues.

Alien had already been in I. for one week when my plane touched down in the early hours of the morning after a delay to the flight. Amid threats and expressions of mutual commiseration, the passengers started releasing their seat belts without any apparent confidence in the obvious fact that they had landed. I noticed my oxygen mask on the floor, where somebody had trodden on it. I kicked it out of the way. With a mixture of embarrassment and guilt I noted that I still had the fingernail marks —a row of livid half-moons—that the woman in the seat on my right had made when she gripped my wrist. As the other passengers started to stand up, most of them yawning or sneezing because of the blast of cold air on the backs of our necks, I looked at the marks: in that dull, aseptic light their nature, shape, and even their color seemed different.

After picking up my suitcase from the baggage reclaim, I walked quickly toward the exit. I immediately recognized Alien's silhouette. She was with her father, who was leaning on the counter of a closed Avis office, talking on his cell phone. I kissed her and gave her father a hug. I noticed that one of his eyes was red, as if he had burst a tiny blood vessel, which accentuated his tired appearance. I looked behind me, and seeing that nobody else on my flight had come through yet, I finally relaxed.

Alien's father drove in silence while she and I stared out of our respective windows in the back of the car, holding hands and entwining our fingers like a couple of teenagers. I had prepared an explanation for the fingernail marks in case either of them noticed: I would say they were the result of the cramped seating arrangements on the plane. Alien didn't notice anything, so I continued to stroke the palm of her hand, exploring with the tip of my index finger an irresistible indentation on her ring. I gave her a summary of my department's end-of-year meeting. Later, as I was recounting a rather distasteful incident that had taken place between two history professors, I heard her father cluck his disapproval.

The road was unlit and Alien decided to engage her father in conversation so that he wouldn't fall asleep at the wheel. He turned up the volume on the radio, and the voice on the radio suddenly exclaimed, "There is no intimacy in a soulless world." One after another, I saw the signs of towns and villages that Alien had told me about in the preceding days. She was keen to visit every spot on the island, even the most touristy and crowded areas. On her first day there, after she had unpacked and had breakfast with her father, we spoke on the phone. I was still marking exams, and I continued scribbling on the exam papers while we talked. She told me that her father wasn't happy. He was dissatisfied with his new circumstances and he felt let down. "You've heard those stories about quiet, stoical loners whose lives are measured out in terms of biological processes such as sleeping, eating, drinking, or whatever?" said Alien. "Well, my father is one of them. But suddenly he's . . . somebody interesting." "How about you?" I asked. "Oh, I love it. I adore this hot weather."

Alien's father's house was a single-story building. Apart from the master bedroom where he slept, there was another bedroom piled high with the belongings of Alien's sister, Inneke, who had decided to stay on in Aarhus, Denmark, where she had been studying on a yearlong Erasmus exchange from her university.

She had told her father that she had a boyfriend there and was now trying to get an extension of her grant so that she could stay and move in with him. We left my suitcase in the bedroom and joined Alien's father in the living room, where he was already dozing in his armchair. The whole place smelt of bleach, but it wasn't unpleasant. The living room window looked onto the well-tended garden belonging to the residents of the condominium, from which we overheard snatches of languid conversations between the neighbors and the sound of several television sets. I wolfed down my tuna salad sandwich with mayo, and we said goodnight.

Intermittently, I remembered the episode on the plane. *Objectively and dispassionately* speaking, it had been exciting. I looked at the marks on my wrist: they had morphed into mauve-colored ciphers.

When we woke up the following morning, we very hurriedly made love (of sorts) in the diaphanous light that filtered through the blinds. After several days spent sunbathing and swimming in the sea of I., Alien's body was warm and supple. The oppressive humidity plastered our hair against our foreheads. Just minutes before, she had emerged from the bathroom and checked that her father was not at home. It was Sunday, his day off. Perhaps he had gone for a walk or to buy the newspaper. Or perhaps he had discreetly decided to leave us alone for a while. We giggled and I persuaded her not to phone her father; she wanted to know what time he would be back. Finally, she put a key in the lock of the street door and, wearing a long winter nightdress that belonged to her sister, she double-checked that there was nobody in the main bedroom.

Afterwards, Alien insisted that we take turns to shower. I was in a good mood, basking in the novelty and relaxation of my surroundings. I pulled up the blinds, and a vivid shaft of yellow light fell onto Inneke's desk. Completely naked, I went into the living room and, assuming a provocative pose draped over her father's armchair, I pretended to watch television; she was not amused.

While Alien was in the bathroom, I returned to the bedroom, put on a bathing suit and browsed Inneke's shelves. Her books, her CDs, her photographs. One of them was of Alien, Inneke and myself a year earlier, on our wedding day. In another photo, her mother—who at the time had been living with the same man for several months—was skiing, grasping two fluorescent ski poles and smiling at the person taking the photograph. There were pictures of Inneke at the top of Machu Picchu with her arm round the neck of an orange-colored alpaca, and another in which she was wearing a voluminous sky blue scarf, leaning on the rails of one of those shabby ferryboats that go back and forth across the Bosphorus every day. As far as I was concerned, the arrangement was far from ideal. Even though Alien and I had been married for a year, we still had to spend our holidays at her father's house like two kids, and not even Inneke was expected to do that anymore. Of the two sisters, Inneke was the one most like their father. She had a boyish, athletic frame, with an almost non-existent waist, and she tended to walk quickly with one hand in her pocket. She was just twenty-two. In a few months I would be twenty-eight. What did that gap of six years mean? (Until then, I had never really thought about it.) I had read most of the books on her shelf, although the last time I read a book with any real enthusiasm, I was her age. But I still listened to the same music. If anything, my taste in music now was even more entrenched. Back then I had imagined that by the time I reached my present age I would be listening to symphonies and going to chamber music concerts . . . that I would eventually conform. Why not, after all? In fact, the only difference between Inneke and myself was that she could still choose. It seemed that I had already made my choice.

Several years later, whenever we stayed with our parents, we would sit down with them at the end of the day and spend the end of our summer holidays with them. We would rummage through the drawers and rake over old fears. And we were no longer shy about them seeing us naked.

When Alien had finished, I went into the bathroom and spread the towel on the toilet lid. I read the contents of some of the medicines placed higgledy-piggledy on a sloping shelf from which hung a small pouch filled with lavender, tied with a bow. Before the water started to flow from the showerhead, I heard the voices of Alien and her father talking in the living room. I stepped into the bath and had an extra-long shower. As I soaped my chest and washed my hair, I thought about what had happened on the plane, and for the first time I felt irritated. Had my passive attitude encouraged the misunderstanding? I'd had an embarrassing erection that wasn't easy to hide. I decided not to mention the incident when I arrived at the airport. It was late, and anyway, it was unimportant. I suppose most passengers started to talk about what had happened (it had possibly been the biggest dose of relativity and randomness they had experienced in years) even before they reached the taxi stand. One of the flight attendants said that in those few seconds the plane had gone into free fall and probably dropped 20,000 feet or more. It was like switching the light off in the garage, closing the door, and then coming back five minutes later for the pruning shears. That unfathomable darkness, that is nevertheless so palpable when we are clumsily groping for the switch on the wall, is what happened up there in the sky. The moment I tried to hang onto the headrest of the seat in front of me, I felt those sweaty, tapering fingers grappling with my wrist and forcing it back down onto my lap. The girl sitting on my right had gripped my hand and was screaming with panic. Minutes after the plane had climbed back to its normal cruising height, she was still clasping my wrist with both hands, digging her nails into my flesh. When I tried to tell her that it was okay, that the danger had passed, she moved closer and placed her trembling lips on mine. The other passengers were crying or stammering out prayers, laughing hysterically, or slumping back into their seats; meanwhile, the flight attendants began to hand out bottles of mineral water. I had simply not reacted. When I finished my shower, I dried myself and went to the living room, where Alien and her father were waiting to have breakfast with me.

The alignment of the house meant that the living room felt cool and fresh in the morning, perfect for walking barefoot on the marble tiles. That morning, Alien's father was quite talkative. I asked him about the new hotel where he was working. He said that most of the guests were English, and he joked about the various wings of the building being distributed according to the total number of tattoos sported by each family. It was obvious that he wasn't happy, but I kept saying how much I liked his new house. None of the furniture was his, except for a few framed photographs and the armchair in which he liked to take his naps. I noticed a climbing plant trained round the top of a mirror in a rattan frame, a material I had only ever seen before in holiday apartments and cafeterias. When he had finished his coffee he lit up a cigarette; from the garden came a sudden whacking noise, the sound of someone belly flopping into the pool. Somebody shouted, "Hey! Nice one!" and Alien and I laughed. Then somebody else let out a long belch. Her father looked toward the window, tut-tutted, and gave us an incredulous look, his eyes wide open and his pupils dilated. I had seen that expression before. Once, before the divorce, Alien's father and I had gotten drunk together. It was all very civilized, one night after dinner as we sat in an old-fashioned wicker swing on the porch of his old house, lighting each other's cigarettes with the ends of the previous cigarettes, like a couple of crooks hot-wiring an abandoned car. As we cleared away the dishes, we asked him if he would like to go to the beach with us, but he preferred to stay at home and read the newspaper. He told us he had bought bread, so why didn't we make some sandwiches and take them with us for lunch. Wrapping the food in tin foil, I said to him, "Last night, when we were driving back from the airport, I noticed a bar with good-looking waitresses. I bet they serve some mean drinks there." He laughed. "How about we go check it out some time?" As we were about to leave, he stood at the door with his hands in his pockets, as usual, and explained how to get to the nearest quiet beach.

"You know what? I think my father has a girlfriend," said Alien as we set off for the beach. Passing a lush border of banana trees, we went through the gate of the residential complex and out onto the dirt road. "Yes, it's a lady who lives two blocks away; she has only one leg. She seems very nice. I think she's the property administrator."

I was still thinking about the one-legged neighbor when we arrived at the beach. Alien's mother was Dutch. She was a difficult, stubborn woman: it was she who had chosen the girls' names. And another thing—she didn't come to our wedding, and since then Alien hadn't spoken to her. You didn't have to be a genius to realize that Alien's father felt he had been left out in the cold. I imagined him making love with that one-legged woman. In better times, sitting on that wicker swing, for example, he would have been the first to make a few witty remarks on a scenario like that.

I had taken along a couple of books from Inneke's bookshelf: J. D. Salinger and Thomas De Quincy. I stretched out on the sand and thought to myself that at least I. was a real holiday destination. There was hardly anybody else on the beach, except for a girl with her dog and a few heads bobbing like glass marbles in the water, its surface dappled with patches of shadow cast by the clouds.

"Are you okay?" asked Alien, taking off her clothes and folding them in a pile next to her cheerful poppy-print beach bag. "Great!" I answered, "And you have a great tan. You're the most beautiful girl on the island." She rummaged in her bag until she had found her goggles and a snorkel. "I mean it." I insisted. "You are the most beautiful girl on the island."

Her father was right, there were a lot of fish at that beach, especially near the rocks. I lay reading on the sand, but I found it hard to concentrate because my mind kept straying back to the incident on the plane the evening before. After that girl had pressed her lips against mine, I said nothing for a few minutes. Somebody was heaving shallow, nervous sighs. There were babies screaming at the back of the plane. The flight attendants were going up and down the gangway with bottles of water that they handed out to the passengers. A man aged about sixty staggered out of the W.C. He was groaning, and his trousers were round his ankles. He had fallen and hit his head on the metal toilet paper dispenser, which was why he was pressing a makeshift, blood-soaked bandage to his head in an attempt to stop the bleeding. After a few minutes, I looked at the girl, but she didn't turn toward me or even seem to notice my movements. She was quite attractive, and younger than me. I was aware of a slight wetness in my mouth in response to the touch of her lips. She must have been about the same age as some of my second- or third-year students. When she stood up, she avoided looking at me, no doubt because she was embarrassed. I had also identified the flavor of her lip balm: vanilla. I hadn't kissed any lips other than Alien's for the last seven years. And even though my feelings for her were unchanged, I realized that this sensation had been *different*.

I started to read and soon fell asleep to the sound of the sea. When I opened my eyes and as I gradually woke up, I tried to spot Alien in the water, but I couldn't see her. I stared at the horizon for several minutes. I waited for her to surface with her goggles and snorkel. I got up and approached the water's edge, hopping to avoid burning my feet on the hot midday sand. I glanced back at my books and the poppy-flowered beach bag next to her towel. When I turned back, I saw Alien smile and wave to a girl who was sunbathing and playing ball with her dog at the far end of the beach. After talking to Alien, the girl stood up. She turned round, looked at the water for a while, and then fastened her bikini top.

I smiled at Alien for a few seconds as she walked toward where I was standing. We didn't take our eyes off each other the whole while. When I thought she was near enough to hear my voice, I raised my sunburned shoulders in a questioning shrug. She nodded affirmatively and quickened her pace, finally breaking into a short run, which concluded in a kiss. "Among all the fishes," she began to say in amusement, "I saw one rather unusual fish." I didn't understand. "It was quite an adventure," she said, breathing out through her nose. Several blue droplets appeared on her chin and trickled down the soft slope of her neck. "Why, what happened?" I asked uneasily. She told me that she had been diving and looking at the fish, a shoal of tiny fish of a strange electric blue color, when a man had also approached to take a look. "I surfaced, removed my snorkel, took a breath of air and said hello to him," said Alien. "After all, there are just a few of us here, and we've all come to look at the same thing…" "And then what happened?" I asked. "I went under again, and when I looked in the direction of the shoal of fish I saw that the guy had pulled down his swim trunks and there it all was in front of me, he was showing off his tackle." I didn't know what to say. I tried to laugh but I couldn't, because she didn't. Alien looked down at her ankles, traced a few squiggles in the wet sand with her big toe, and went on: "I told the girl over there that there was a man exposing himself in the water." She stammered for a moment and made a funny face: "His thing had been operated on, *it was rolled back*. I'm not bothered, but some people might be shocked," she added. "Anyway, it wasn't very nice, to say the least."

I waded in up to my waist and scanned the surface of the water to see if I could make out the figure or shadow of a man. Then, suddenly, I looked at her, as if the episode had somehow left a mark on her body. "Don't worry about it," said Alien, "he swam away, so he's probably on another beach by now." "Did he say anything to you? Did he have a beard?" I asked. "No, nothing, he just looked at me. Actually, he seemed slightly jumpy, like a little boy. Then he made a weird, yelping sound." I really didn't know how to react to what Alien was telling me. I looked at the girl at the other end of the beach: she was no longer topless, but she was still playing on the sand with her dog, which seemed used to splashing about in the sea and resolutely swimming in pursuit of its ball. “Let’s forget about it.” she said. “I’m ravenous!” She strode back to her towel, looking at the ground the way her younger sister did. She took the sandwiches out of the bag, unwrapped hers and tossed mine to me with a hollow smile. I sat down beside her and kissed her bare shoulder. “Are you okay?” I asked her. There was a sound of excited barking. I turned round and saw the tennis ball flying through the air and a cloud of sand being kicked up by the dog as it ran. “Fine,” she said over her shoulders, “just don’t tell Dad. It would only upset him.” I nodded in agreement. Then she popped the tab on her can of soda and started to drink.

# MIDNIGHT SUN

As Heikki closes his mouth, his thin lower lip brushes against the short, prickly hairs at the edge of his moustache, stained a copper color by the smoke from his cigarettes. He begins to mouth an answer to the referee, or perhaps to himself; it is the most basic physical response to a random thought that suddenly makes us aware of something. But the right answer never comes. In another kink in the linear, coherent train of thought, the silent gesture gives way to an irrepressible urge to urinate a vivid yellow stream, which dispels the distressing thought of a half-finished building.

The landscape surrounding the lake at dusk, with its palette of greens ranging from the unnaturally green lawn, as if it had been sprayed that color, and the pale hue of the tops of the polar fir trees, gives way to a view of scaffolding pockmarked with rust, uneven pyramids of rubble and an out-of-tune radio playing somewhere under the ladder.

This hyperborean scene effectively disproves that the ether is separate from the ground. Now, at the height of summer, it is as if everything is happening inside the iridescent spiral in a glass marble, where it is always day. A glass marble in which the pungent, clean but invisible smell of ozone triggers adjacent areas in Heikki and Tina's brains.

On the television set that Heikki has taken out of the cabin—an old black-and-white Grundig with no remote control—the Argentine referee has just blown the whistle for the end of the first half, with his right arm extended and his fingers closed, pointing in the direction of the luxurious locker rooms, the ultimate dream scenario of every advertising agent marketing any brand of men's underwear. But, from where Heikki is sitting, the referee is pointing to the far edge of the lawn behind him, about sixty feet away, toward the dappled surface of the water and the dark birches on the far side of the lake.

When he stands up, the nervous twitch in his right knee stops. Like a scene in a Tarkovsky movie, Heikki's heavy body moves slowly along the wooden table; he turns a rusty chair round, putting it back in its usual position, and turns the volume dial on the television set to the left. He wanders dreamlike around his improvised outdoor living room, a transparent sky above him and a carpet of cool, damp, night-illuminated lawn underfoot. Just like in his early childhood games, Heikki has constructed an ephemeral, precarious house that will only last as long as the football match. Or until Tina decides it is time to take all the furniture back inside. Because the game is over. Because there's nothing else worth talking about tonight.

He quickly walks down to the birches and fir trees by the lake, where the gnarled roots break through the grass and surface here and there. Tiny drops of dew tremble as the rubber soles of his boots, about a size twelve, come to a halt beside a bare patch of black earth in the cool grass. Suddenly, he catches a glimpse of a fish jumping out of the water. Thanks to the subtle glow of the Finnish summer solstice, the variety of greens is breathtaking. The green soaked greenery in a greener green (Nabokov). The lingering light gives the cabin and the lake, as well as the silence, which is only broken by the occasional wave rolling over the surface of the water, the translucent quality of a canvas held up against the light.

Heikki reaches the small jetty raised on concrete pylons that juts out into the lake. Another golden-scaled fish emerges for a few seconds. From there,

Tina's pitch-roofed log cabin, which appeared smaller from a distance, looked more like the hut of a paraplegic forest ranger, which it probably was before she lived there. Tonight, in fact, there are two houses—Tina's cabin and the other one: Heikki's short-lived, makeshift, ephemeral house. Without the dining table, the three straw-bottomed chairs, and an old-fashioned sideboard on which he has stood the television set, the cabin is empty. If the TV were turned off and the succession of images stopped flashing on and off the screen, it would seem as if the heart of the forest had suddenly dried up.

After a few minutes, Heikki feels a hot tingling sensation in his urethra. Meanwhile, he waits with his fly open. He undoes the fasteners that hold up the denim bib and makes an awkward grunting sound, which somehow matches the color of his moustache, and the earth soaks up the slithery stream of his alcohol-bleached urine. Then, Heikki's robust body quivers slightly from his waist to his forehead, for a moment investing him with a kind of vulnerability, although there is nothing ingenuous about him. Staring at the purplish head of his penis (curved and prominent like the eye of a cartoon character which has popped out of its socket in amazement) and the space between the arms of the V formed by his boots at the water's edge, Heikki returns to what he had been thinking before he was interrupted by the referee: *This is Zidane's big night, as long as the fates smile on him. I just know it is going to be Zizou's night, even if he is playing in black and white.* At the same time as he catches a glimpse of another fish leaping out of the water, a thought originating in some place in the brain that is impossible to pick up on an X-ray (just as Heikki's soul could never be captured on photographic film) enters his mind like an underground spring flowing into a lake: *Everything is possible. Any situation can become normal. Here I am again, as usual, hardly giving it a second thought, all washed up, without a drop of semen.*

He goes back to his chair, to his ephemeral house under the sky, inside the glass marble. The chair legs are slightly bowed forward because of the damp. He is waiting for the broadcast to be resumed from the Olympic Stadium in Berlin; the twenty-two players are still off the field. Heikki opens another beer. Then he wipes the cold sweat from the can off the palms of his hands. On the bare table there is a bottle of vodka, five large crushed beer cans, two pieces of peach in syrup floating beside three cigarette butts in a souvenir dish from the Åland Islands, and a white, blue, and green cap emblazoned with the name of his mechanic. There are also two crumpled twenty-euro bills that he is going to leave for Tina.

In less than two hours from now, the midnight sun will roll out a new July day inside the glass marble. The slightest movement will cause a faint glimmer in the orb. Progressing a little further into the iridescent spiral, it will be the first of the 1,460 days during which Italy or France will reign supreme over world football. From the stool where she sits operating the sander on the porch, Tina watches the stiff, rigid movements of Heikki's body. He is sitting quietly absorbed in the game. Every so often, he crosses his leg over his knee and fiddles with his bootstrap. He looks right at home in his outsized playpen. Like an innocent child. One who doesn't yet have wet dreams.

Heikki is her best client, and when he comes to stay she earns good money for her work. She busies herself with the household tasks while he watches her, talks to her, discusses whether a player was offside, or amuses himself building a house on the lawn. Today he's watching the 2006 World Cup final. *The poor guy has no semen*, Tina thinks to herself, *but it's better that way. She would give anything for him to get it back. Where can he have lost it? In what dark corner of his addled head can he have buried it? Today she will have to leave early.* For all his forty-two years of age, Heikki still can't get his head round the fact that night and sunlight can coincide. Or that a man can have no semen in his body. He looks tired. She goes on sanding. In a little while, a few circles of sawdust are piled up on the windowsill beneath the transparent sky, inside the illuminated bell jar.

But Heikki has just leaned his furrowed forehead against his clenched fist. It is *the universal sign* of despair in a man. Looking at the TV screen, Tina sees that Zidane has just been sent off, which seriously damages the chances of the French team in this final. The TV camera lingers on the numbed, apologetic face of player number 10 as he heads toward the locker room—everything is the color of ashes on this old Grundig, lending the whole scene an aura of a bygone age: it's as if everything had already happened, or had never happened at all. Zidane's teammates look at each other, and Heikki starts muttering at the screen, like it represented something that had to be smashed to pieces.

"It isn't the screen's fault," says Tina, unplugging the sander.

(And anyway, since when is *Monsieur Sans Sap* a freaking French citizen?)

"So, where did my semen go?" thinks Heikki.

It is almost midnight when Tina finishes sanding the shutter on the porch. Everything is green in this World Cup light, as green as sulfur smoke. She unplugs the machine. She looks at him. *That's why he sometimes thinks of himself as a half-finished building.*

*That terrible year 2001 and all that godawful stress . . . It's like when you're staying in a place that's being renovated, and you don't really feel you know what the building is like. It isn't the same building anymore, but a building under construction. He isn't Heikki anymore; he is the man without semen, even though I'm the only one who knows.* There is still something on the TV, but Heikki has fallen asleep with his arms folded on his chest, worn out by stress and the lack of vital sap. Is it because he is getting old? He's starting to get a few small brown warts on both his eyelids, and his eyebrows look thicker and straggly. The two twenty-euro notes that Heikki left for Tina (who went inside the cabin a few minutes earlier) are lifted and blown onto the lawn by a passing breeze. Only the dazzling round disc of the sun is reflected on the surface of the lake, whose occasional gentle ripples are the reverse image of the lines scored by the blades of skaters on the ice in winter. Sensing that he is alone, Heikki slowly wakes up, gathers his things, and leaves. He walks away from the green. Without seeing another gleaming fish jump out of the water, *blighted sun scrotum* between the ether and the ground.

# DUALITIES IN A THREE-STAR MEDITERRANEAN SUNSET

Tiny flashes of white light sparkle on the crest of a wave that rolls on and on, seemingly never to break, indifferent to the sea around it. The light is a mellow orange color. In fact, that cloud is exactly the color of a segment of exceptionally luscious tangerine. The air is warm, in harmony with the temporary respite from low pressure and humidity. In the distance, the cloudscape is tinged with the hues of both evening and morning light. The few clouds in the sky are cirrus, thin as morning mist, and look like the fossilized remains of the plumage of a prehistoric bird; they could be drifting or simply disintegrating. As she stands facing the sparse landscape, the old woman with a Dutch passport who has come out onto the balcony of her hotel room is struck by the fleshiness of this time of day: her name is Ria, she is eighty-one years old, and she lives with her husband on the outskirts of

Breda. It is an in-between time, a time of transition, but one that is repeated every day during the summer season. Depending on the latitude, on how far north or south you are on the Mediterranean tourist coast of Spain featured in the travel agency catalog, it occurs around nine or half-past nine. Ria takes several deep breaths of the salty island air. It's as if the day were straining to overstretch itself, like a taut bow made of some indestructible material. As if—just this once—night, hunger, and sleep would never come. It is the moment when dogs—always true to themselves—bark at the retreating sun. Leaning against the railing, Ria sips her gin and tonic; it will take her three days to familiarize herself with the surroundings. The predominant colors are: the green of the pine branches, the turquoise of the water, the velvety orange of the clouds, and the soft mauve of the sand on the beach opposite her. A fundamentally warm range of colors, instilling in her a profound sense of physical well-being and an acceptance of the twilight of experience.

Ria rests her arms on the sharp edge of the railing, which is still warm from the afternoon sun. Meanwhile, she waits for her husband to emerge from the shower. During the holidays, this is the only routine there is: the warm touch of the sun on her freckled, liver-spotted skin; occasional dips in the sea; the appearance of sudden crops of varicose and spider veins; open windows and curtains; gin and tonics; an excursion on a catamaran and performances by local vocal groups around the pool. Since she arrived, Ria has eaten nothing but the Ritter Sport chocolate bars that she bought at the airport. She continues to gaze at the scene, savoring under her tongue the pale blue bitterness of the gin mixed with the iodine in the atmosphere.

The beach opposite is deserted except for some youngsters who, in the eyes of the elderly woman, configure an essentially hermetic group. The procession of British and Central European couples making their way to the restaurant finished some time ago. Ria has observed that it begins around seven in the evening and finishes at half past eight. She puts down her glass and, on closer inspection, she sees that the lone group on the beach has just re-created the image of one of the Mansions of the Moon. To be precise, it is a moving, man-sized replica of Lunar Mansion 21: two men, one of whom is turning his back to the other, while the other is facing outward. Next to them, another man, who has cut their hair, is collecting it, or rather showing it to one of the young men, whose long locks have been replaced by a patchy, close-cropped haircut. The image is not at all faithful or strictly accurate, and it isn't as sharply defined as it could be, owing to the jerky, erratic movements of the two young men, who are now pelting each other with pebbles and wet sand, impervious to the weather and the fact that it is fall. There is also a woman, whose sudden appearance jars with the essentially masculine nature of the hermetic scene.

(It is not until the third Mansion of the Moon that a female figure appears: magnificently attired and seated on a comfortable chair, her right hand raised above her head, while her left hand tugs at the hair of a madwoman who is trying to get away.)

The girl is not very splendidly dressed, either (all she is wearing is the bottom part of her swimsuit), nor is she trying to run away, escape, or disappear; in fact, she goes and joins the group of boys.

Meanwhile, Ria's husband has come out of the bathroom and is sitting on the edge of the bed, getting ready. The colors in the room are dark and subdued. Outside, it is still sunny.

The girl lies down, spreading her hair on the upper corner of the towel (where there is a sprinkling of yellowish-beige sand). Through some imperceptible connection between her synapses, she becomes aware of the sand. Paying no attention to the loud laughter of the three boys, she gets up and walks to the water's edge. Bending over to form a perfect ninety-degree angle, her bust level with her slim hips, she carefully rinses her hair in the water from the roots to the tips. After wringing it out over her right shoulder, she removes the elastic band encircling her biceps like a Sioux body ornament and uses it to gather her damp hair into a short, compact ponytail. They are all tanned from their exposure to the sun all summer long on afternoons just like this. They probably live on the island, Ria concludes. And their skin is an earthy color, like wet clay.

Ria leans on a plastic chair. It is like those you see in cheap, unpretentious Spanish terrace cafés. Her gaze moves back and forth from the car park on the east side of the hotel to the little cove where the hermetic group of youngsters has gathered. The fabric of her cheerful summer outfit, with its violet, white, and blue stripes, peeks through the slits in the back of her chair, the openings revealing a sequence of colors and shades like a bright zoetrope of her ageing kidneys. Offering the basic amenities of a summer resort hotel, the room has a short passage leading to the bathroom, and there is just enough space for the bed, a bedside table and, about a foot from the end of the bed, a television and a remote control on a cabinet against the wall. Under the television there is a gaping space about the size a seven-year-old child's back, where the wall is water-stained from some leaky old mini-bar that is no longer there. The mirror reflects a reverse image of the whole room, including the sweeping sea horizon depicted in the watercolor hanging over the double bed.

Her husband is still sitting there. He pulls on his gray socks, and only then does he slip on a pair of dazzling white leather sandals, which leave the top of his feet exposed. Over the years, fatty cysts have formed all over his legs, small swellings like half ping-pong balls, threaded with tiny, pale veins. As he adjusts the Velcro strap round his ankle, the muscles in his arm firm up. It is the only time that the blurred outlines of the anchor, the chubby impish little Cupid, and the Feyenoord football club logo tattooed on his forearm are able to get the better of his wrinkles. His tattoos have long since lost their definition. With the passage of the years, the fine and bold lines have given way to a succession of tiny dots the size of the tip of a ballpoint pen. In the long corridor of Ria's memory, the thin film of salt and moisture dispels any grudges born of past infidelities and betrayals.

The group forming the twenty-first image of the Mansions of the Moon has climbed to the top of the small slope overlooking the cove. As they walk, their feet kick up a few stones in the gravel lot used as a parking area by the hotel guests and the occasional visitors to the tiny cove. When they get into a red sports car, the elderly woman shifts her interest to two figures that have just emerged from between two cypresses; they have very likely arrived in that beat-up old crate, which certainly looks nothing like a *rent-a-car.*

Ria sees a child and an adult walking in concentric circles, as if they have lost their bearings: aimless, concentric circles. The boy is clutching a shoebox to his right side. The elderly woman's attention focuses against her will on this new visual stimulus. She needs to know who these people are. A mixture of piquant curiosity and inexplicable joy rushes through her brain. Her husband has come out onto the balcony; his right knee creaks. He is drinking another gin and tonic from one of the glasses they found hygienically wrapped in plastic covers in the bathroom on their first day. They have shared absolutely everything for the last forty-five years, although their gestures no longer mean the same or have become meaningless: he goes to stroke her belly, an insignificant gesture that has no bearing on their future. She draws his attention to the two strange figures, and she feels the renewed, damp shadow of blood between her legs. Before he reminds her that they need to go down to the swimming pool if they want to get seats for that evening's show, she is so caught up in the moment that she cannot tell whether it is the child or herself (after thirty years she thinks she is menstruating again)—that is acting out his or her true role in this here and now.

The rough cardboard box is chafing against his side. On one corner there is a triangle of insulating tape, the point of which is so sharp that it has pierced the delicate skin of one of his fingertips. The child isn't squeamish at the sight of blood. He casually sucks the wound without saying anything to his father. Only after the sports car has pulled away and he is given the signal do they walk on. At the same time, the boy catches a glimpse of a woman's eyes, which disturbs the rhythm of his breathing.

In spite of his father's explanations, the child interprets the tinkling of the bell coming from inside the box as renewed signs of life or stifled calls for help that only he can understand. It is quite heavy. He feels a little light-headed from all this aimless wandering about. Now that night has fallen, the only thing that betrays the dilapidated presence of the old Opel Kadett is the faint sound of the radio coming from the dark interior of the car. On their short drive to the cove, the boy had gazed at the sun setting over the landscape. Meanwhile, his temples throbbed with the last heat of the day mingled with the smell of the cracked vinyl upholstery. Everything flashed past. Thanks to the compliant law of inertia, his neck wobbled as if constantly nodding in assent. He is familiar with the route: during summer vacation he travels along it every day, both on foot and on his bike. It is the distance that separates the quiet residential area where he lives with his parents from the small cove, where elderly foreigners with hairless, white legs go swimming in the sea. He is thinking that the box, although not actually empty, in reality is empty. It is a complicated thought. It's like when he was on the highway and inside the car at the same time; the box is both empty and not empty. The only way he can grasp anything is to remain in a vague, cloudy haze. He doesn't know if he feels sad. At home they have a communal garden, shared by all the residents, so his father said they would have to go to the plot of land next to the nearby hotel after dusk. They had driven there so as not to meet anyone on the way. A short distance beyond the fenced parking area, they come to the clump of pine trees. Night has continued to fall the way it does in folktales, in all the pre-Christian myths, and in some forests; or maybe like in the distant memories of a real-estate agent suffering from cancer, very, very slowly. By doing it at that time, his mother said, they would avoid being seen by anybody they knew. But, now that there is no daylight, it is impossible to judge where it would be best to bury the box. Besides, the ground is very stony.

The father begins to dig several feet away from the boy. His moving shadow is a little lighter than the color of the sea at this time of night.

"You can't see anything from here," the boy says suddenly. "If somebody from the hotel parks their car here, it will block the view of the beach."

To his right, his father leans on the handle of the shovel and pauses to catch his breath. He looks right and left and right again, making sure the coast is clear. He hesitates for a moment and motions to the boy to keep well clear of the area where the cars are parked. There are pebbles and gravel everywhere, and sinking his shovel into the ground is more difficult than he had anticipated.

"But Moose didn't poop here," the boy insists, pointing toward the slope leading down to the cove. He used to do it *over there.*

The father agrees to dig next to the last pine tree before the wooden fence. It is dark now, and the only faint light is from the full moon and the lamp strung from the branches of a pine. The long, twisting roots of the tree, extending a dozen feet or so under a pale mantle of flickering light, appear to be the only thing holding the clay soil of the slope above the cove in place. The murmur of the waves mingles with the sound of music drifting over from the hotel garden, and the tiny wildflowers growing among the stones are all atremble. There are lights on some of the hotel balconies.

Having recently discovered sex on the Internet, the boy's imagination conjures up female bodies concealed behind the curtains of those illuminated balconies that punctuate the darkness. Not even the sinister tinkling of the bell on the flea collar can stop his erection. There is nothing he can do to prevent it, and even though the darkness would conceal the little bulge in his pants, he only feels more embarrassed; so he bends forward in the hope of creating a bit of slack at the crotch.

But his father is bound to notice his strange behavior and reprimand him for walking like an animal, or waddling like a duck.

The hole is dug.

The boy helps his father to fill the grave with earth. As he does so, he thinks of the inside of the box dropping into the hole. He imagines a big dragon curled up within the four cardboard walls; he imagines it beginning to lumber majestically through a rocky wilderness of dry cactus plants and stubble. Running along the dragon's back there is a row of fierce-looking triangles reaching as far as the flea collar. In the distance there is a craggy hill, which at the same time is a volcano. From the crater gushes a copious jet of clean, transparent water, which floods the entire plain. The motionless dragon is submerged—the fleshy triangles on its back gently swaying like seaweed or jellyfish—at the bottom of a soothing, crystal clear sea. Then the boy has a terrifying idea: "What if they build another hotel on this land?"

The father responds with a long, drawn-out silence. He seems to be mentally counting the recent building projects in the area. The cove is the same as always, enclosed on one side by the restaurant and by the hotel gates on the other. The hotel isn't new; it has been open at least twenty-five years. What's more, if he is not mistaken, this is a protected area. He tries to allay his son's fears and goes on filling the hole with earth. Nevertheless, this new fear leads the boy to imagine a Caterpillar excavator chewing up the soil and the trees, the stones and the bushes in its enormous jaws. Among the slag, ash, pebbles, and plastic bags full of un-degraded tin foil, he sees the damp folds of the cardboard. The box has become a blackened, soggy mass bulging at the corners and invaded by mold and maggots. Inside, the boy imagines a sort of giant hair comb made of rib-shaped bones crowned with several brittle, worm-eaten triangles.

When they have covered the hole, the boy and his father stand looking at the ground for a long while without speaking. Then the boy picks up some stones and rocks that are lying around him and arranges them in the shape of an M. One of them is polished so smooth and flat that it would be ideal for skimming and might bounce as many as five times on the water. The boy and his father stare at the ground, but they can hardly see a thing. Holding their arms out before them, they feel their way back to the car, taking care not to stumble. In the pitch black, the two cones of light from the front of the vehicle project a stereoscope of superimposed yellow lines on the road. As they drive away, the boy has already decided that he will go back to find out what has happened inside the box. All he can hear is the sound of the waves on the shore.

That wave did finally break, after all. And the only light is from the landing gear on the fuselage of the planes flying overhead in the darkness, like specks of astral debris glimpsed through the branches of the pine trees. As in the (slow-motion) dreams of a sick animal, the sound of the sea can be heard but not seen, engulfed in the subtle harmonies of 1960s British pop music. Everything is superimposed on everything else in the clepsydra of time: sadness and sex, death and dream, rest and sand. And so it goes on, always and forever, under the influence of the moon and the passing summers.

# A BRIEF THEORY OF TRAVEL AND THE DESERT

The world has turned full circle. Now it revolves around a car that has just dropped off a Russian hitch-hiker.

"I don't like Almeria," Ben grumbles from the front passenger seat, aware of the lingering taste of gasoline under his tongue. "My father's car had an Almeria license plate. I always thought it was crap."

Ben and Magali are willing captives of the vast desert landscape of Almeria, but their nerve endings remain trapped between the riveted partitions of the restroom at the gas station, the first stop on this journey that began at a place that could have been anywhere on the Costa del Sol. It's July.

(Although Ben and Magali speak the same language, right now communication between them is faltering.)

After several hours driving parallel to the Mediterranean, passing a succession of Muslim torsos bent in morning prayer (religion wedged between speed bumps and grimy car washes) and the sprawling sea-front mansions flashing past them, they reached the desert and the gas station that they have just left behind: an oasis of asphalt, broken glass, and plastic.

Ben looks at Magali. She is beautiful. He looks at her firm, skinny arms resting on the wheel, the arms of a willowy music conservatory student, and all the while he has the tune of "Woman Driving, Man Sleeping" by Eels ringing in his ears. Through the windshield, the horizon shimmers in the heat, like when a child plucks at water in a glass.

Minutes earlier, at the gas station, Ben had been unnerved by a volley of high-pitched electrical sounds from the loudspeakers: it was as if they heralded the impossible ringtone of a gigantic mobile phone crouching behind a limestone hill, the shadow of some monstrous creature from a *hentai* or *anime* cartoon (the product of his imagination set ablaze by the stifling midday heat of Almeria). The stench of fuel and burning rubber hung in the air as far as the bend in the road where the hitchhiker coolly walked away, haloed in sheer nothingness, as if in a country music video. Because, as Ben instinctively knows, *the one to blame for all this* is the Russian hitchhiker they picked up back at the traffic circle and just dropped off at some godforsaken place on the map—any map—showing Almeria. (He hadn't even said goodbye when he got out of the car.) What's more, the description of the beach he'd recommended to them was probably a perverse Soviet lie.

First hypothesis: Anyone who is heading for a desert—Magali, Ben, or that hitchhiker—is running away from somewhere else.

The detour just taken by the Renault Mégane, described in such profuse detail by the Russian hitchhiker, is a narrow road leading to the coast. In Ben's mind, it's as if the arid, dusty scrubland it runs through were an extension of the gas station's wheezing machines, barrels, and oil drums, its cables and cans reeking of fuel. It's been years since he has seen any of these old milestones, cement bollards with a red semicircle painted at the top. (These are not the only visual cues on the journey that will remind him of his childhood: his father meeting him every day at the school gates carrying a green plastic bag, the tips of his father's fingernails scorched and stained yellow by his cigarettes.) The cement and asphalt of the road are riddled with cracks. Ben gazes at the piles of sand, gravel, and ballast, the cement mixers, slag heaps, storage drums, gasworks, pumps, and transmission towers as they fly past. The horizon shifts and changes like a nightmare scripted by some master of destiny in a science fiction movie who unleashes all sorts of insane behavior in the other characters and whom Ben doubtless identifies with the Russian who has just got out of the car: the unfailingly loyal, consummate *garde du corps* of some despicable Hollywood hero. For a moment, Ben wishes he weren't in the vehicle, which he now associates with a bad dream. He wishes he could get out and go back home, he wishes he were sitting in his father's beaten-up Peugeot with its Almeria license plate. If only he could wake up, damn it!

*But Magali . . .*

It had been *her* idea. *She* was the one who had invited him along on this trip. After exchanging a few inconsequential words that had lifted each of them out of their respective states of loneliness, *she* invited him to travel the Spanish coast with her. Anyone watching them now—the Russian hitchhiker, for one—would think, "They've quarreled and are not talking to one another." Or, "They're a couple of weirdoes who get their kicks by making other people feel uncomfortable. But she's very attractive, *strangely attractive* to be traveling with an awkward, self-absorbed guy like him. And another thing, that scar on his head . . . It gives his boyish face a more manly look." But in fact, there is a much simpler, even prosaic explanation. Ben and Magali don't know each other (even though from the very first day they talked in the park and Magali invited him to join her, Ben has felt as if he has *always* known her: a good enough reason to lie to his father, telling him that he was going on a trip with a few of his buddies. He had reassured him, saying he had all his medication with him, and told him not to worry).

Ben begins to feel more anxious as Magali, her forehead beaded with perspiration and tired after driving so many miles, accelerates on a perfectly straight, seemingly endless stretch of road. Or rather, it would be endless if the driver's natural inclinations had anything to do with it. "That Russian devil," thinks Ben. "Until he turned up, everything was fine, but now we are both haunted by him in this place from which there is no return: the desert."

The Almerian desert.

As Ben grips the handle above the side window on his right, the possible implications of the scene burst chaotically on his imagination. Amid the swirling clouds of clay dust and particles of gravel thrown up by the pressure of the four wheels spinning at high speed, and through the sparse clumps of vegetation that could be thyme, anise, or just plain weeds, Ben's burning eyes spot a large, intact dentist's chair in a gently reclining position resting on a rusty metal base, in amongst the bushes. Its white enamel is made all the more dazzling by its contrast with the two russet-colored rocky outcrops framing the far distance. The imperious noonday sun creates the illusion that the dental lamp is turned on. The frame of the chair is aluminum and, under the leather chair back, an articulated arm is connected to a tiny pipe that delivers water to wash away the patient's blood after an extraction. (Ben remembers a photograph of Marilyn Manson, his large teeth crudely exposed by a dental device consisting of metal rods and bolts, some of them rusty, wearing an SM Nazi leather aviator's helmet.) The object is so powerfully charged with multiple layers of meaning that Ben cannot tear his eyes away from it, even when the dentist's chair has receded into the distance (into what now looks like a field of sunflowers) and he can only watch in the rearview mirror until it finally disappears. He continues to gaze at it until the marine blue of the beach finally looms into view (and he comes to the conclusion that there will always be something causing a gap, an imbalance between her and himself).

Second hypothesis: the desert is, by definition, an arid, uninhabited, strictly impersonal space, perfectly in tune with the deepest levels of the human psyche.

The silhouette of the Russian hitchhiker evaporating in swirling clouds of dust and light was the last human form they saw through the car windows. But . . . He was right. The beach he had told them about really did exist. Magali is finally driving into a parking area surrounded by a picket fence, a gravel-covered slope that they will have to climb carrying the umbrella and the straw beach bag that are stowed away in the trunk along with Magali's beloved violin.

Magali locks the car with her remote control and walks up the embankment without saying a word.

Ben hates the Russian. Why on earth did they take pity on him back at the gas station? He says the first thing that enters his head to stop her thinking—if that is what she's doing, as he fears—of the darned hitchhiker:

"Do you feel like taking a swim, the first swim of the summer?"

Ben still can't see anything. At first, he thinks there is nobody on the beach, but then he notices a guy of about fifty who looks like a security guard: he is fat, has a moustache, and is smoking in the sun, which increases the sensation of heat in Ben's head. He slyly makes as if to turn round as Magali passes by, but Ben's piercing stare stops him in his tracks. As they start their descent toward the water, a playful little dimple appears at the side of Magali's mouth. In scarcely a few hours, Ben has learnt that she always somehow remains aloof from the world around her (whether it was this beach in Almeria or the frenzied ducks on the pond where they first met. She was crying. *It was her tears that made him hers.*) Now Magali could not be further from crying; she walks purposefully at first and then races idiotically like a child onto the sand.

"There's one little thing our friend from the former Soviet Union didn't tell us, don't you think, Ben?"

Several seconds go by before he makes the connection between her words and what his eyes can see either side of him on the beach: a profusion of bare buttocks, breasts, and pubic triangles, and a rusty placard indicating that they are on a nudist beach. He notices that the fence is lined with dark canvas to discourage any potential voyeurs from the area. Ben, of course, has never set foot on a nudist beach before. He wonders if Magali . . . But no, he doesn't dare ask her, fearing as he does the only possible answer.

Now they are on the beach, surrounded by naked bodies, and he calculates without looking at Magali—whose shadow on the sand has come to a halt—how long it's been since he last immersed himself in the sea. While he is thinking, without looking at her, he can sense, he can *feel* as if it were engraved on his retina, Magali's translucent naked form stretched out on a cotton towel. He prefers to gaze at the shoreline, focusing on the gradations of amber that are finally interrupted by the ribbon of foam on the sand. Seen in the light of the bloody prism suspended in the vault of the heavens, the sea takes on a rusty, reddish hue, as if the father of Venus had just had his testicles cut off and cast into the waves. Never once looking at Magali, he walks toward the swirling sea. His penis is as before: icy cold, motionless, timid. The heat has built up in his head and now he bathes, performing an ablution that is half running away, half initiation rite. He opens his eyes and looks at the beach through a wet gaze like that of a crocodile placidly gliding along in the water; the legs and arms of the people strolling, sleeping, or reading on the beach, oblivious of the heat, seem to multiply in the distance. The water is very cold, but not cold enough to cool the ball of fire that is lodged behind his eyes. He shuts them, but he forgets to shut his mouth as he ducks beneath the water, and the sea salt that enters through his bodily orifices traces in his mind a network of roots connecting him to a primeval aquatic world: a world suspended between nothingness and life. Flooded with all these sensations, prompted by the petrified taste of salt, a channel carved by fire in his DNA chain forges a path through the waves: there is saliva on his tongue and he feels hungry. The feeling is located not in his stomach, but a little higher, near his windpipe, where the particles of salt slowly penetrate and finally quell the hunger, drowning out any new thoughts.

*From there, gently rocked by the waves, the child can see his mother: she has got up from her folding chair in the shade of an umbrella bearing an ad for non-alcoholic beer. Her hair falls over one side of her still pale but very beautiful face. With the eye that is not shaded by her hair, she looks up and down the long beach as she adjusts her flowered bikini top edged with petals. She is a long way from him, but the child knows that she is watching him; he knows that his mother is about to head in his direction. Next to the chair she has left vacant, there is another empty chair with rusty-looking legs that are sunk firmly into the sand. She paddles in the water and waves to him. His mother is carrying a small shiny package wrapped in carelessly crumpled tin foil, proof that somebody has taken a peep at its contents, decided they didn't want it, and wrapped it up again. The child remembers a multi-grain roll filled with several slices of salami. His mother smiles as she hands him the sandwich and his whole being is flooded with salt and sea. She turns round, and, instead of sitting down again, continues walking at an unhurried pace; when the child looks up from his afternoon snack, the two chairs are empty.*

Somebody has opened Ben's eyelids to talk to him. It is Magali. She has removed her full, dry lips from Ben's. He can feel fingers—soft delicate fingertips—holding his eyelashes and opening his eyes so that the light floods in. It is so dazzling that his first reaction is to turn his face to one side and shelter his eyes from the sun. His momentary blindness contrasts with the perfect, absolute clarity of his auditory perception. He can tell exactly where the voices around him are coming from. The light. The light is white, Ben thinks to himself. And she has chosen me. From somewhere behind his head, which is resting on the soft sand, he can hear the crackling sound of an old walkie-talkie, but over and above all the other sounds he can hear Magali's voice, saying there's no need to worry.

Somebody is saying that it might be a case of sunstroke or stomach cramps.

Ben reflects that he has never felt better. His back feels cool, a feeling that spreads through his body and finally puts out the ball of fire in his head. In fact, he feels neither hot nor cold—the two sensations cancel each other out—and he keeps his eyes shut. He has forgotten about his naked body and the tiara-shaped scar on the top of his head, his skin has turned to sand; he is aware of the water around him and the singular, silent presence of Magali.

They start to talk, but Ben doesn't open his eyes. He is lying face up. He is aware of her moving to his right. As Magali tells him what has happened, their feet intertwine and the sand slides softly over the top of Ben's foot. She is saying that they'll spend the night at the nearest campground so that he can get as much rest as possible.

The journey has only just begun, this very instant. And the Russian, Malaga, the gas station: they're the lumpy vomit spewed out through the cracks in this broken world.

All the while he has been gently nodding; a soft breeze caresses his chest, his abdomen and (he is reminded of it by a quiver caused by the nearness of Magali) his anemic-looking penis. But I feel fine, says Ben, shakily, and he opens his eyes to see hers looking at him. He sits up, and what he now sees (Magali's pure white body) is exactly as he had imagined it would be.

(*I must phone my father, he's going to feel lonely while I'm away*, Ben thinks, closing his eyes once more; the world turns full circle again, and Magali's back slides into the water.)

Final hypothesis: Our souls are empty, but they need movement.

# ABOUT THE AUTHOR

CRISTIAN CRUSAT (1983) was born in Spain, the son of a Spanish father and a Dutch mother, being himself both Spanish and Dutch. He is the author of *Estatuas* (Statues) *Tranquilos en tiempo de guerra* (Peaceful in times of war) and *Breve teoría del viaje y el desierto* (*A Brief Theory of Travel and the Desert*). He has seen his essays, translations and articles on literature published in a wide range of Spanish and Latin American journals. In 2015 he published his latest collection of stories in Spain, *Solitario empeño* (Solitary persistence), to great critical acclaim.

## ABOUT THE TRANSLATOR

JACQUELINE Minett teaches Translation and Interpreting at the Faculty of Translation and Interpretation of the Universitat Autònoma de Barcelona. She was previously lecturer in Modern Spanish Poetry and Drama at the University of Durham. She translates from Spanish, French and Catalan into English.